SWAT
Secret World Adventure Team

New York
City

written and illustrated by
Lisa Thompson

PICTURE WINDOW BOOKS
Minneapolis, Minnesota

Editor: Jill Kalz
Page Production: Tracy Kaehler
Creative Director: Keith Griffin
Editorial Director: Carol Jones

First American edition published in 2006 by
Picture Window Books
5115 Excelsior Boulevard
Suite 232
Minneapolis, MN 55416
877-845-8392
www.picturewindowbooks.com

First published in Australia by
Blake Education Pty Ltd
CAN 074 266 023
Locked Bag 2022
Glebe NSW 2037
Ph: (02) 9518 4222; Fax: (02) 9518 4333
Email: mail@blake.com.au
www.askblake.com.au
© Blake Publishing Pty Ltd Australia 2005

Printed in the United States of America.

Library of Congress Cataloging-in-Publication Data
Thompson, Lisa, 1969-
New York City / by Lisa Thompson ; illustrated by
Lisa Thompson.
p. cm. — (Read-it! chapter books. SWAT)
Summary: Ari and Tess are recruited by the Secret World
Adventure Team for a mission in New York City, where they
visit many well-known sights while trying to win a contest
that may save an amazing roof-top skateboarding park.
ISBN 1-4048-1670-4 (hardcover)
[1. Adventure and adventurers—Fiction. 2. Skateboarding—
Fiction. 3. Contests—Fiction. 4. New York (N.Y.)—Fiction.]
I. Title. II. Series.
PZ7.T371634New 2005
[E]—dc22   2005027166

Table of Contents

SWAT

DESTINATION PROFILE

NEW YORK CITY

*DESTINATION: New York City U.S.A.

CURRENCY: US

*POPULATION: 8 million

*LANGUAGE SPOKEN: English (New Yorker Style

*MAJOR LANDMARKS: Empire State Building, B
Statue of Liberty, Central Park, Su

*Hottest weather in: August

*Coldest weather in: January

Visitors per year: 17 million

Number of Yellow Cabs: 11,000

Also called: The Big Apple

S.W.A.T. I.D.
AGENT No 0
CODE

SOUVENIR OF VISIT TO THE
Empi
(17556
9810

MADISON AVENUE

West 74th

8th AVENUE

MAP OF MANHATTAN - NYC

Hudson River

Upper WEST Side

Central Park

El Barrio

Upper EAST Side

CHELSEA, the Garment District and Times Square

42nd St to Central PARK

Greenwich Village

EAST Village

Lower EAST Side

Queens

Soho

Chinatown and Little Italy

Financial District

Civic Centre

Brooklyn

MAP OF MANHATTAN - NYC

5th avenue

MOST FAMOUS BUILDING IN THE WORLD

A SOUVENIR OF 1931

EMPIRE STATE OBSERVATORIES

0645894

ellis Island

OBSERVATION DECK- Statue of LIBERTY

New York City is made up of 5 boroughs - Manhattan, Brooklyn, Queens, The Bronx and Statan Island.

Chapter 1
The Mission

Ari and Tess had been skateboarding hard all afternoon, practicing tricks and monster airs. Ari picked up speed and launched himself high into the air. Turning mid-flight, he grabbed his board with one hand and the edge of the ramp with the other.

"Awesome invert!" yelled Tess.

Suddenly, Ari missed the board on landing and hit the ramp hard. Thud!

"That was a bone crusher," moaned Ari, lying on his back, his board still rolling back and forth next to him.

"Ari, move it! You're blocking my way!"
Tess shouted. She wanted to launch one
last time before calling it a day. Ari
crawled off the ramp to make way for
Tess. It was then that he noticed the
strange brown package.

"Hey, Tess, is this yours?" Ari asked.

Tess finished her moves perfectly and turned around. "No," she answered.

"Well, it was next to your bag, and it's got both our names on it," Ari said.

Tess walked over to check it out. "It wasn't there before. I wonder how it got there."

A cell phone lying under the package started to ring. Ari picked it up and pressed it to his ear.

"Tess and Ari, welcome to SWAT. What I am about to tell you is classified as Top Secret."

"It's for us!" Ari said excitedly. "Tess, you have to listen to this."

Tess pressed her ear to the other side of the phone. The message continued.

"I am the voice of SWAT. My name is Gosic. SWAT is a top secret team whose name stands for Secret World Adventure Team. We have a database of every child in the world. From this list we choose our special agents. Congratulations! You have been chosen for our next mission. We urgently need your help in New York City.

"Your mission is to help TJ and his friends save their skate park. You have 24 hours to complete this mission.

"Inside this package are two SWAT transporter wristbands. You must wear these wristbands at all times. They allow you to travel in the blink of an eye, and they keep us in contact.

"Keep these hidden, and tell no one about SWAT.

"You must leave at once! Press **START MISSION** on the transporter to begin.

"Good luck, SWAT."

The phone went dead.

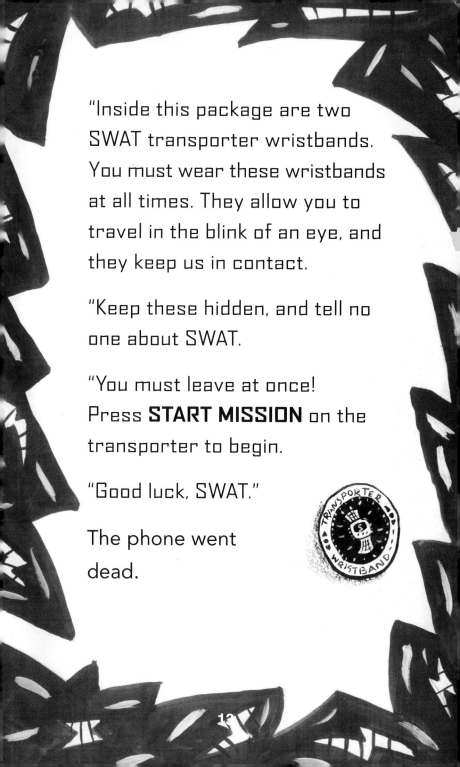

CHAPTER 2
New York City

"I can't believe this is happening. New York City, here we come!" Ari grinned. He scanned the mission notes while trying to put on his wristband. "This TJ looks like a great skater. He can do a 360 ollie, kick off a ramp, and go down a flight of stairs!" Ari handed Tess a photo of TJ.

"I don't know if I can go," said Tess softly.

"What!" Ari almost dropped to the floor. "What do you mean you can't go?"

"I've got an assignment due tomorrow. I haven't even started it," she said.

Ari threw his hands up in the air. "Tess, we're going to New York City, and we don't have a lot of time."

"But I don't know anything about the place!" she protested.

"What do you want to know? New York City is the largest city in the United States, and it's divided into five main areas—Manhattan, Brooklyn, Queens, the Bronx, and Staten Island."

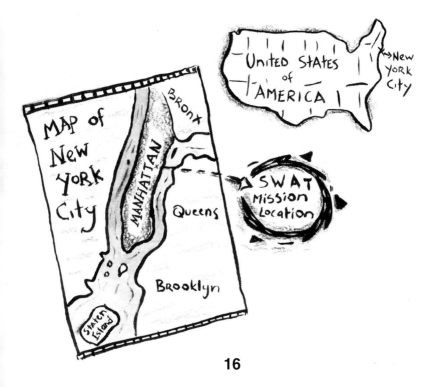

Ari continued, "People from all over the world flock to New York City for fame and fortune. Think big buildings, like the Empire State Building and Rockefeller Center. Think rap music, hip-hop, jazz, cool art, yellow taxis, graffiti, and all kinds of people in the street. Think baseball teams like the New York Yankees and the Mets.

"New York City has to be the most amazing place in the whole UNIVERSE! It's fast, big, and exciting."

"Ari, you never fail to amaze me!" Tess said. "How do you know all of that?"

"You're not the only one with a brain around here," Ari said. "I do read. It's just that I don't like doing my homework."

Tess held out her arm, and Ari slipped on the wristband.

"Trust me, Tess. You're going to love New York City. We'll skate up the ramp, count down from three, and press the **START MISSION** button. Three. Two. One!"

Click.

Ari and Tess landed on a very different ramp. They were on the rooftop of a tall building in a sea of tall buildings.

"No way!" Tess said as she spun around to stare at the skyline. "This place is absolutely MONSTROUS!"

"Welcome to New York City," said Ari, "the city that never sleeps."

They scanned the skyline, and Ari pointed out some of the famous buildings. "That pointy tower is the Empire State building. That one with all the curves and spikes at the top is the Chrysler Building. And look, there's Rockefeller Center. Almost 250,000 people go there every day."

"That's huge!" Tess could barely believe it.

They both leaned over the edge of the building to watch the crowds and traffic crawl through the gridded streets.

Ari turned around to look at the ramp and the rooftop they were on. He couldn't believe his eyes.

He tugged on Tess's arm to get her to turn around. When she did, she let out a slow and shocked, "NO WAY! Is this for real?"

"Tess, if we weren't in New York City, I'd have to say we were seeing things. But we're here, and this is definitely real."

The whole rooftop looked like a dinosaur
park of twisted metal. All of the ramps and
jumps were disguised as creatures and
strange, twisted shapes.

The place was like a steel zoo and a skate park all in one. A kid was skating on one of the ramps.

Chapter 3
Meeting TJ

"I bet that's TJ," Ari said.

Ollies, inverts, monster airs ... TJ could do them all, and he was better than anyone Ari and Tess had ever seen.

Ari started skating off the ramp shaped like a huge dragon. He did a couple of ollies and airs, and he even did the new skating trick he'd been practicing all afternoon—a switch frontside flip.

"You skate pretty well," said TJ, walking over. "I haven't seen you around here before. I'm TJ." TJ spoke fast.

"Hi, I'm Ari, and this is Tess. A friend told us about this place. We thought we'd come and check it out. Cool setup."

"Yeah. It's a shame we only have it for another couple days. The building is going to be sold. Some development guys want to buy it and demolish the skate park," said TJ, looking glum.

"They can't knock it down. There's nothing else like this in the world. It's unique! It's the coolest place for a skate park I have ever seen," Ari said.

"Yeah," said TJ. "You'd never think there'd be something like this on a rooftop, but here it is! When you go up off the ramp, you can see for miles. The guy who used to own the building was a sculptor who loved to skateboard. That's why all of the ramps and jumps are so cool. Now they want to turn it all into expensive apartments."

Ari shot Tess a glance and said, "We can't let this happen. This skate park is awesome."

Just then a boy came running over.

"Meet Carlos," said TJ.

"Hey, TJ, you're never going to believe this," said Carlos. "The radio station 324NY is running a competition. The prize money is the same as the price of this building!"

"No way!" said TJ. "What do we have to do? Skate to the moon?"

"The station is going to announce three clues," said Carlos. "Each clue will lead to a mystery item hidden somewhere in New York City. Find all three mystery items, and the money is yours.
The competition begins at noon, and there's a new clue every four hours."

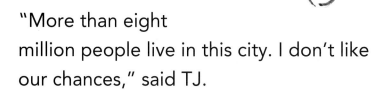

"More than eight million people live in this city. I don't like our chances," said TJ.

"But we have to give it a try!" Tess piped in.

"You're right," said TJ. "OK, Carlos, go round up the others, and we'll all meet at Lucky Lou's in half an hour. Let's go, guys. We've got tons to do."

Chapter 4
Lunch Meeting

TJ led Ari and Tess to a little shop. The man behind the counter was yelling at the top of his lungs. Above the door hung a sign that read:

The shop was packed with people, none of whom seemed to notice the shouting.

All sorts of strange and delicious smells filled the air. Pastrami hung over the counter, and bagels lined the shelves. A lady dressed in black was making the biggest, most mouth watering sandwiches Ari and Tess had ever seen.

The lady started hurling questions at TJ.

"Where have you been?" she began. "How's your mother? You haven't been getting into any trouble have you? Who are your friends? What's happening with the skate park? Are you going to have something to eat?" Then she turned to the shouting man and said, "Hey, Lou, go and serve TJ."

The group piled into a little booth at the back of the deli, and Lou came right over.

"This is Lou," said TJ. "He's the rudest waiter in New York. If you don't order quickly enough, he'll order for you."

"Hurry up! Hurry up! Stop wasting my time!" shouted Lou.

Ari started to say something, but Lou had already ordered for them. He grumbled his way back to the kitchen, his hands waving all over the place.

In a flash, Lou was back with a plate as big as a tray.

"BLT burger with eggs over-easy, fries with extra red, three frozen strawberry cows, six flapjacks with syrup, and a little something extra to go," shouted Lou, as he dropped the plate onto the table.

"What did he say?" asked Tess. She hadn't understood a word. TJ pointed to the plate.

"We have a bacon, lettuce, and tomato burger with eggs, french fries with extra ketchup, three strawberry shakes, pancakes with maple syrup, and some cookies for later," TJ said.

Carlos came in, followed by two others.

"Jenny and Rick, meet Ari and Tess. They're going to help us win the radio competition," said TJ, as he made room for them to sit down.

"OK. Here's the plan," said TJ softly. They all huddled together. "The competition starts in one hour. We'll split into pairs and head for different parts of the city. When we work out where the clue leads, someone will be close."

Everyone nodded.

"Jenny, you and Ari take midtown. Rick and Carlos, you guys go uptown and stay around Central Park. Tess and I will stay downtown," TJ said. He reached into his bag. "Everyone gets a phone and a radio. We'll all listen to the clues, and whoever solves it first calls the pair closest to the site. Now let's eat!"

Chapter 5
Clue Number One

At exactly noon, the first clue came in over the radio.

"I am a woman who stands clutching a flaming torch. I live alone on an island and am monstrously tall. I was a gift from France and arrived in the United States in 214 different crates in 1884. For many new Americans arriving by ship, I was their first glimpse of their new country.

"The seven points on my crown radiate to the seven continents and the seven seas. Come over and visit me. Somewhere in my crown lies a torch waiting for you to find."

The clue wasn't even finished, and TJ had worked it out. The phone began to ring. The others had worked it out, too.

"I know, I know!" yelled TJ over the phone. "It's the Statue of Liberty! Too easy!" He turned to Tess. "Quick, Tess, this one is ours. We have to catch the ferry to Liberty Island NOW."

They skated at lightning speed to the wharf, catching a ferry just before it left. "I hope you're in good shape, Tess, because climbing to the top of the statue is like climbing a 22-story building," said TJ.

When they reached Liberty Island, the pair ran past the crowd and headed straight for the narrow, spiral staircase.

They climbed for what seemed like forever, squeezing past people, huffing and puffing. Near the top it got really hot and claustrophobic. Tess made a final dash past a lady wearing an "I love NY" T-shirt who looked as though she might pass out.

They reached the top and burst through the door with their last bit of energy.

The torch was hidden above a viewing window and wrapped in a red ribbon marked "Congratulations." Tess and TJ grabbed it. It was nearly 10 minutes before the next person ran through the door.

"Sorry, Bro," said TJ. "Too slow!"

Once they caught their breath, Tess and TJ walked around to take in the awesome view. It was windy and cold. Tess could see all over Manhattan.

"I can't believe I'm standing in her crown!" she exclaimed.

TJ called the others to tell them. Tess could hear cheering on the other end of the phone. Then it was time to walk the 22 stories back down to the ferry.

Chapter 6
Clue Number Two

Clue number two came over the radio at exactly 4 P.M.

"I play all day and sometimes don't make a dime. Crowds rush past like they don't have time. I can do the tango, I can sing the blues, and I could do the Watusi dance if I had the shoes. Sometimes I play on the corner of 45th and 3rd. I've acted on Broadway—I played a bird! Today I'm playing in the biggest park in town. I'm the one playing the piano and not making a sound. On the top of my piano is a copy of today's paper. Read the bold headline, and you'll know the caper."

Carlos and Rick were already thinking.

"He's a street performer somewhere in Central Park," they said. "That's the biggest park in the city, but where in the park? It's huge, and which guy is he? Hundreds of people perform in that park!"

The phone rang. It was Jenny. "He's in the middle of the park near the Bethesda Fountain. I saw him this morning. He's a mime artist, and his piano has a huge candelabra on it. Hurry guys," she said.

Rick flicked his board high and ollied down a flight of stairs. Carlos followed. They made a beeline for the park, past a team of firemen rescuing people from a smoke-filled building and the crowd watching. They flew past a blur of restaurants, offices, news stands, barber shops, clothes shops, and delis.

They passed graffiti-covered walls and people selling hot dogs from pushcarts. They zoomed down streets and hopped over potholes. They skated right past police officers directing traffic and almost made a little old lady drop her groceries. They took a left turn into the park.

They skated through the hundreds
of joggers,

in-line skaters,

bike riders,

dogs,

and strollers

that filled the park's
many walkways.

There were groups of people everywhere, gathered around performers who were singing, dancing, doing magic tricks, and telling jokes. There was even a DJ with a huge sound system playing the coolest dance music.

"I love that DJ!" Rick yelled to Carlos, as they flew by.

They turned right, then left.

"I see him," cried Carlos. "Split up, and come in from different directions. Cut that guy off on the bike, and I'll grab the paper," yelled Rick.

Carlos slid along the grass, and the bike rider lost his balance. Rick threw himself at the miming pianist.

Rick grabbed the paper from the top of the piano and unrolled it. It was a copy of the *New York Times*. The headline read, "Congratulations, Winner of Mystery Item Number Two!"

"Yeehah!" cried Rick, as he gave Carlos a high five. "Only one more mystery item to go and the skate park is ours."

But they didn't stay still long. A curly-haired in-line skater was so jealous of their win that he chased them for miles—almost the full length of the park!

They finally lost him and called the others. They arranged to meet on the steps of the New York Public Library.

When the boys arrived, Ari and Jenny were already there. They had taken the subway and were sitting between two giant marble lions. The four of them sat down and waited for TJ and Tess to arrive.

Ari told them all how Jenny had taken him around Times Square and along Broadway. They had also taken two elevators up to the 102nd floor of the Empire State Building and had looked over the city.

"I felt just like King Kong," joked Ari.

Finally TJ and Tess arrived, and they all waited for the third clue.

Chapter 7
Clue Number Three

The third clue came in at 8 P.M. The Manhattan skyline glowed.

"If you're in a pickle, sometimes the only solution is to eat your way out of it, no matter how big the barrel!"

"That's it?" cried Ari. "That's the clue?
What does that mean? No one's going to
guess that!"

"This competition is rigged!" Ari huffed
with disappointment.

The rest of them sat there with blank faces.
Who would ever figure out that clue?

TJ kicked the ground.

After a long silence, Tess said softly,
"Joe's Pickles."

"What?" asked TJ.

"Joe's Pickles," said Tess again. "You
walked me past it today. I remember
asking you about them because there were
all of these barrels out in front, and you
said Joe's pickles are famous in New York
City. People come from all over to eat a
pickle out of the barrel. The third item is in
one of the pickle barrels. I'm sure of it!"

TJ leapt to his feet.
"We'll have to take the
subway." He led the way
on his skateboard, and the
others followed. "We'll get off at
23rd Street. Joe's is on the corner of
5th and 22nd. Let's go! We have to get
to those barrels first!"

They flew around street corners. They
barely noticed the crowds and the noise
of the city. They rushed through seedy
back alleys and along busy roads, past
warehouse apartments, hotels, offices, and
people standing in doorways.

When they got there, Joe was standing out front with two barrels. No one else was there—yet.

"I wondered who'd guess it first," said Joe with a smile. "You have to bite into all of the pickles in the barrel to find the one with the mystery item in it."

TJ turned to Jenny and Ari. "OK, guys, it's your turn."

Ari and Jenny bit into 243 pickles. Finally, Ari yelled, "Ouch!" Inside the pickle was a gold coin with the radio station's phone number on it.

"We did it!" shouted Ari. "We found all three mystery items. The prize money is ours! We saved the park!"

Ari jumped up and down. TJ gave him a
high five. Carlos, Rick, Jenny, and Tess
were all jumping around, flipping their
skateboards in the air. Even Joe got in
on the fun.

A crowd had formed around them, and everyone was cheering. There were film crews and camera flashes. Cabs on the street honked their horns. Everyone was yelling, jumping, and dancing. Then the people from the radio station burst through with a giant check. The skate park had been saved!

Suddenly, Ari and Tess felt their SWAT wristbands vibrate. They looked down to check the message:

Congratulations! Well done, SWAT! Mission return.

Chapter 8
Let's Celebrate

The next day, TJ and the crew were in all of the newspapers. They didn't have to climb the fire escape to get to the skate park anymore. They owned the building!

Lucky Lou's had a party, and the whole neighborhood was invited up to try the skate park. Everyone came. Even the angry in-line skater from Central Park showed up. It was a great mix of people.

When no one was looking, Tess and Ari
slid away to a ramp in a quiet corner of the
rooftop. Their wristbands were flashing.
The message read, "MISSION RETURN."

"It's time to go," said Tess. "I'm going to
miss New York City. I was just getting used
to the people and the crowds. It really is a
city where anything can happen."

"We have to ask Gosic to send us on another SWAT mission," said Ari, picking up his new skateboard.

"Where did you get that?" Tess gasped.

"TJ gave it to me. The color's called
'pickle green.' Cool, huh? But this is one
SWAT agent who no longer eats pickles!"
said Ari. He took off and did a perfect 360
ollie kick.

"Such style!" cried Tess.

"I got it in New York City!" said Ari.

Tess laughed and shook her head. "I'll count us out. Ready? Three. Two. One!"

Ari and Tess launched off the ramp.

Click.

MISSION RETURN.

Glossary

bagels—round breads that look like donuts

beeline—a direct route

candelabra—a fancy candlestick

claustrophobic—afraid of closed-in spaces

clutching—holding tightly

demolish—to pull down; to destroy

glimpse—a brief, quick look

hurling—throwing with force

inverts—to turn upside down

midtown—the middle of town

monster airs—lots of height between the skateboard and the ground

monstrous—huge, oversized

pastrami—smoked beef, usually eaten in sandwiches

radiate—to move outward from the center

seedy—shabby, dirty

subway—the New York City underground train system

switch frontside flip—a move in which the skater flips the board over with his front foot and switches front feet before he lands

360 ollie—a move in which the skater slaps the tail of the board down hard, jumps, and spins fast so the board grips his feet, and he does a circle in the air

Empire State Building
NEW YORK CITY

Ships can be seen
40 miles at sea

73 elevators operate at
speeds ranging from
600ft. to 1,200 ft. a minute.
7 miles of shafts

6,500 windows to wash
on a continuing basis

3,500 miles of telephone
and telegraph wire

50th floor

60 miles of water pipe

One of the world's eight
wonders (The only one
built in the 20th Century)

20th floor
10th floor

World's greatest TV
tower - 1,454 feet

Used by TV stations
in the metropolitan area.
Reaches 8,000,000 TV sets
in four state area.

Visibility on clear day
80 miles

102nd floor observatory
(1,250 feet up)

86th floor observatory
(1,050 feet up)

1,860 steps
from street level to
102nd floor

60,000 tons of steel-
enough to build double-
track railroad from
New York to Baltimore.

Over 2.5 million visitors
from every state in the
United States and nearly every
foreign country
visit "Top of the Empire State"
each year

Volume of building
37,000,000 cubic feet

Thousands of post cards
sold annually

2,248,000 square feet
of rentable area

Site of John Thompson
Farm, 1799

PLAYBILL IN-LINE

The
Museum
of
Modern
Art

IT COULD BE YOU!

Secret World Adventure Team

COME TRAVEL TODAY!

A complete list of *Read-it!* Chapter Books is available on our Web site:
www.picturewindowbooks.com